THE BIRD WITHOUT WINGS

Deborah Burggraaf

1.20.16

dburgg.com

Protective Hands Communications
Riviera Beach, Florida

ISBN 978-0-9818990-9-1
Library of Congress Control Number 2009908353

Published
By
Protective Hands Communications
Riviera Beach, FL 33404
Toll free: 866-457-1203
www.protectivehands.com
info@protectivehands.com

Printed in the United States of America

Dedication

For the kids in my life...

Ryan, Eden, Robert, and Barry

and to

Officer José Cuellar, who gave me Cooka.

Once, there was a bird; a green Quaker Parrot without wings.

She was called, Cooka.

Cooka spent her days looking out a big window from her cage inside her Florida home.

She watched the puffy, white clouds blow across the blue sky.

She watched the lizards climb on the window each day.

But Cooka was not happy.

Cooka wanted to explore the outdoors and discover new things.

She wanted to play in the grass and feel the sunshine on her body.

But Cooka had no wings!

How could she go outside to play?

One day, Cooka's cage door was left open.

Cooka used her sharp talons and sleek beak to climb out of her cage.

"This is amazing!" Cooka thought.

"I can go outside to play!"

Cooka peeked outside and lowered herself to the bottom of the stand.

Holding on tight with her sharp talons, she reached the bottom of the window sill.

"Oh, the breeze feels so warm and fresh on my face!" exclaimed Cooka.

Cooka managed to hop down onto the cement of the patio deck.

Ka boom, Ka boom! She landed, but did not flutter, because Cooka did not have wings.

Cooka shook off the harsh landing with her head and smiled.

"I did it! I did it! I can now go out and see the world!"

Cooka waddled side to side in the moist Florida blades of grass.

She came across a huge red ant hill, where everyone was busy building their home.

"Why do you work so hard?" she asked.

"We make our own home together," replied the red ant. "We are very small and it takes long hours of team work to build our home."

Cooka grinned and was happy. She watched the trail of busy red ants in the warm Florida sunshine.

Cooka felt each blade of grass as she glided through small ponds from the afternoon rain in Loxahatchee.

"These look like lakes!" she called out, as she met a white Ibis searching for bugs in the murky water. "Hello, my name is Cooka. I see you are very busy."

"This is lunchtime for us," shared the Ibis. "Following the afternoon showers, we find our meal for the day. Would you like to join us?" offered the Ibis.

"No, thank you," replied Cooka. "This is my day to discover the world outdoors," she said with a smile. And Cooka hobbled off.

Cooka, the bird without wings, continued her journey.

She walked and walked and walked.

Next, she came upon a huge red barn and from above, she heard a shriek.

"Shree…Shree!" cried the owl. "Shree, Shree!"

It was a mother Barn Owl perched in the window.

"Sh…sh…be very quiet. I'm watching my nest of babies as they sleep during the day."

Cooka quietly whispered goodbye and headed for the canal behind the barn.

The canal was full from the rains and this indeed, was a lively spot.

Across the pasture were birds and frogs and even horses.

Cooka waddled from side to side as she approached the edge of the canal.

"Oh, you slither so sleekly through the swampland," said Cooka as she greeted the Southern Ringneck Snake.

"Yes, we search for snails and slugs and bask in the warm rays of the sun," replied Mr. Ringneck.

“It has been hours since I left my home next to the window,” Cooka shared.

Mr. Ringneck Snake offered several snails for Cooka to try, but she frowned.

“I usually eat crackers, apples, and seeds all day,” she said.

Just then, Mr. Ringneck Snake found some Sea grape berries for Cooka to nibble.

“I think I’ll try this,” she gleamed. “Thank you!”

The two enjoyed lunch together as the sounds of the wildlife were music to Cooka’s ears.

Cooka, the bird without wings, was still ready to explore.

She thanked Mr. Ringneck Snake for the midday treat as she glanced into the rippling canal.

"The frogs are having a party!" exclaimed Cooka. "I think I'll join in!"

"Clack, clack, clack, rack, rack, clack, clack," the frogs croaked in harmony.

They each welcomed Cooka to their lily pads.

"This lily pad will hold you just fine," assured Mr. Pig Frog. "Just hop on!"

And with that, Cooka, the bird without wings, joined in the frog party.

Just then, in between the sweet songs of the frogs, lumpy lids with eyes appeared on top of the soft water. A long body with rough, brown skin surfaced, facing Cooka straight on. The American Alligator's eyes did not blink, as his large head rose from the depths of the canal.

"This is lunchtime for the alligators. It is not good to be in the water now!" clacked Mr. Pig Frog.

Cooka, the bird without wings, had now floated out to the middle of the canal on her lily pad.

"What can I do? I cannot fly! How can I return to the edge of the canal?" Cooka cried in fright.

"Surely, I will make a tasty lunch for the alligators," she added.

"Someone, HELP! Please help!" Cooka pleaded.

Cooka, the bird without wings, was frightened.

She could not fly and was now trapped in the middle of the canal.

"Help, please help!" Cooka insisted as Mr. Alligator approached her lily pad.

The frogs tried to offer Cooka a vine to take hold of in order to bring her to safety.

They pushed and pulled and pushed and pulled, but it was no use.

Cooka, the bird without wings, was floating in the middle of the canal.

Cooka began to shake.

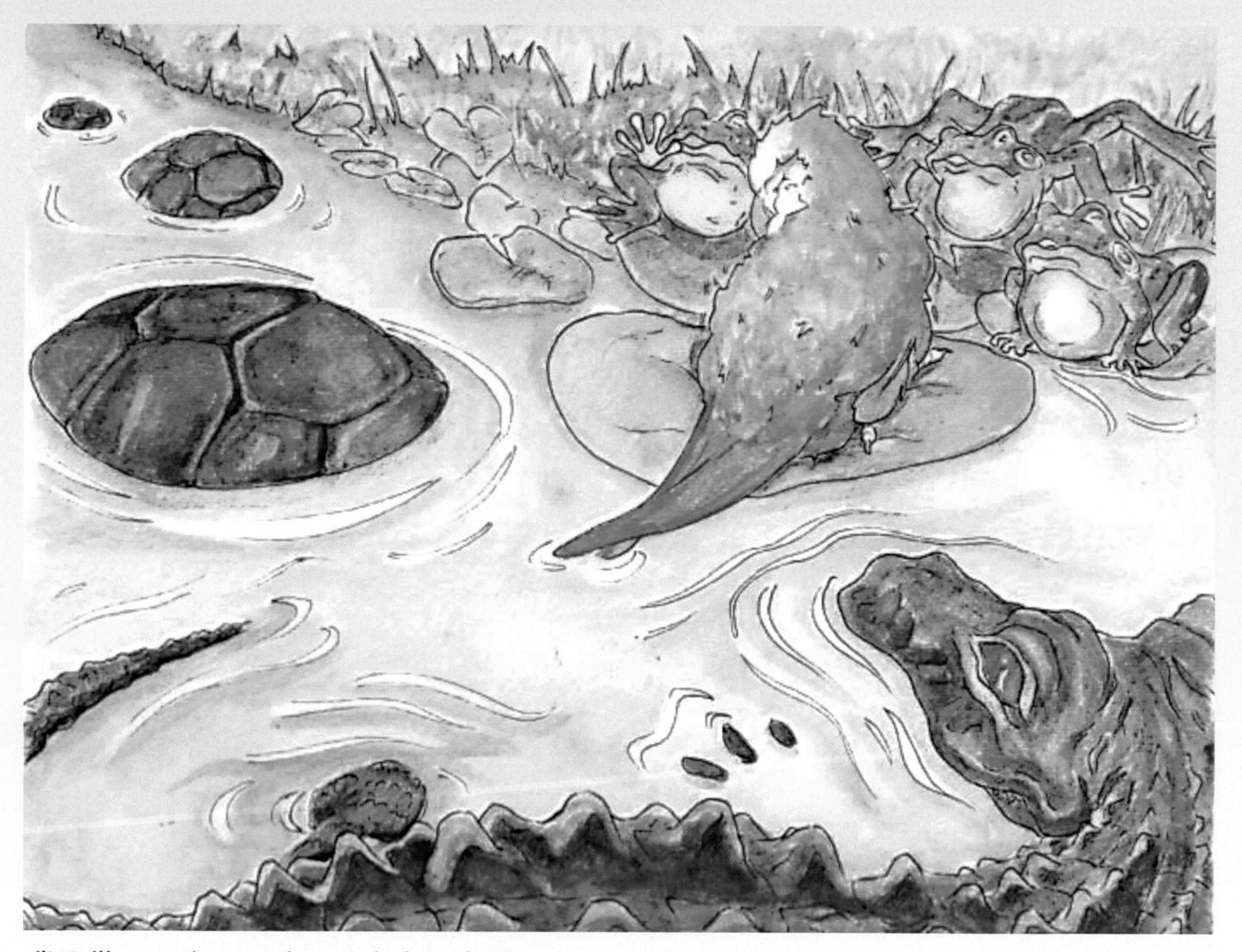

"We'll get the turtles to help us! They can carry you across the canal to safety," clacked one baby frog.

"You can hop on the turtle's hard shell and you will be lifted to safety," offered Mr. Pig Frog.

All of the frogs began to sing their tune in order to get the turtle's attention.

"Clack, clack, clack, rack, rack, clack, clack," they boasted across the canal.

Just then, the turtles appeared from under the surface of the water.

Mr. Alligator's body was in full view now as Cooka quivered.

"Hurry, hurry!" ordered Mr. Pig Frog.

"We don't have much time! We need your help fast!"

"We need you to carry Cooka to safety, or she will become Mr. Alligator's lunch!" warned the frog.

Cooka, the bird without wings, longed to be home in her Florida house crunching on crackers and diced apples.

Mrs. Red-bellied turtle commanded, "Cooka, just hop on my hard shell and I will paddle you to safety."

Without hesitation, Cooka stretched her long neck.

With her sleek beak and sharp talons, Cooka grabbed hold of the hard-shelled turtle. She climbed on top and cried in relief.

Mrs. Red-bellied turtle paddled and paddled.

She carried Cooka across the canal to the edge of the water.

Cooka looked back to see the canal waters calm in the afternoon heat.

Mr. Alligator had submerged himself and retreated.

Cooka, the bird without wings, was now safe.

"Now, I will bring you home," offered Mrs. Red-bellied turtle.

"I think you have had enough excitement for one day," shared the turtle.

"It will be a very long trip as I walk slowly. We will not be home before dark."

"Hold on tight, Cooka," she suggested.

The afternoon clouds had built a dark, gray house in the sky.

The summer rains in Loxahatchee began to fall in large drops, hitting the ground like slivers of diamonds.

The two made their slow journey home.

They walked and walked and walked. They enjoyed the sweet scents of jasmine mixed with the summer rains.

An orange and red blanket draped the sky providing warmth for their voyage home.

Dusk softly set upon the two friends.

Cooka waved good-bye to her new friends and said farewell for today.

She chirped back to her new frog friends.

She said good-bye to Mr. Ringneck Snake.

She said good-bye to the Barn Owl.

She said good-bye to the Ibis family.

And she said good-bye to the busy red ants, who were still busy working on their home.

Darkness set upon the two as they approached the house.

Cooka and Mrs. Red-bellied turtle reached the cement of the patio deck.

"You are now back home, Cooka," chimed the turtle, out of breath after such a long crossing.

Cooka, with a tear in her eye, thanked her new friend.

"Thank you for helping me to get back home. I couldn't have done it without you! Please come back to visit me."

"I know we will see each other soon," Cooka cried.

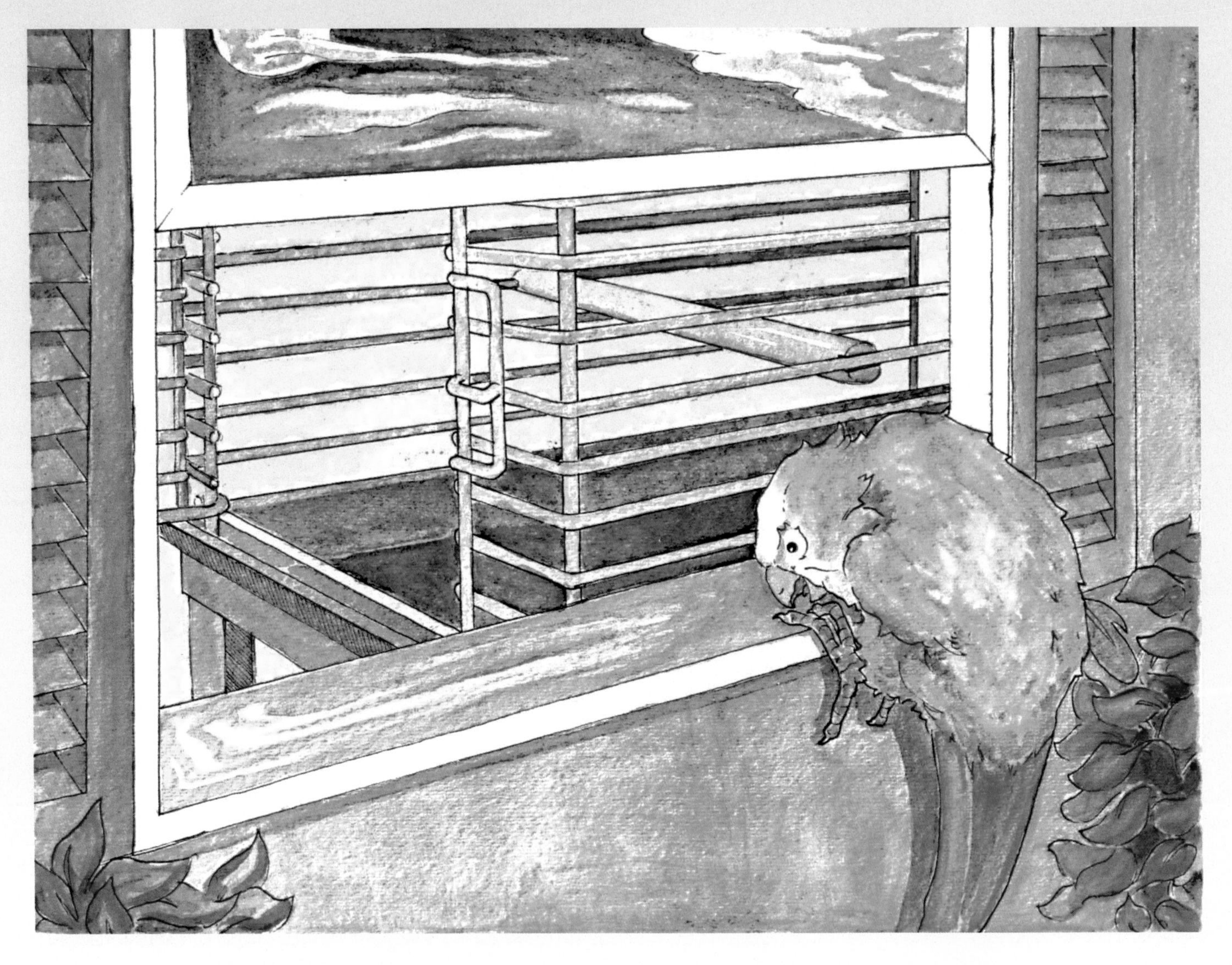

Cooka, the bird without wings, hopped off Mrs. Red-bellied Turtle's back.

Again, using her sleek beak and sharp talons, Cooka climbed up to the familiar window sill.

The door to her well-known cage was still open.

Cooka, the bird without wings, was happy to be home.

Cooka was happy she had explored the outdoors.

She was happy to have made many friends.

She was happy to have experienced the excitement of the day.

Mostly, she was happy to have discovered that anything is possible, even for Cooka, the bird without wings.

Deborah Burggraaf's first picture book came about after she began taking care of three birds rescued from a nest that had fallen from a tree. **Cooka** is Deborah's Quaker Parrot that has only one blue feather with limited use of her short wings.

Deborah is a sixth grade teacher who believes that reading picture books to students develops a lifetime love for reading. She resides in Palm Beach County, Florida with her family, two dogs, three crabs, turtles, fish and of course, Cooka.

Shaun Howard is particularly known for his exquisite use of watercolor with landscape and animals. **Cooka** is Shaun's third picture book.

Shaun has dedicated his life to illustrating children's books. He captures the story with his vibrant color, artistic design, and playful animals as each page comes to life.

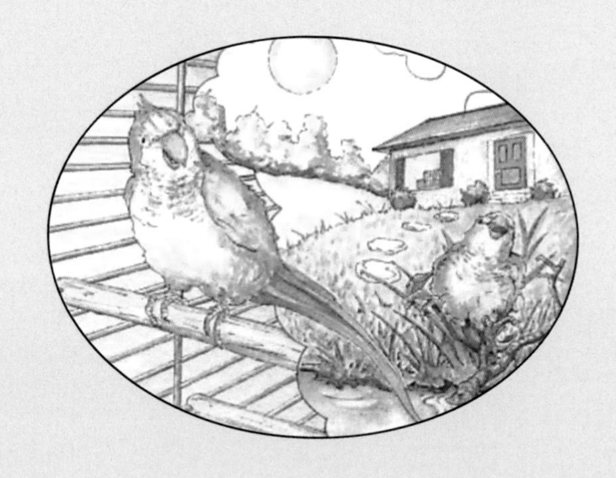